بود بازرگان و او را طوطی ای

در قفس محبوس زیبا طوطی ای

The Parrot and the Merchant is based on a tale from *Masnavi*,
one of the best-known and most influential
works by Rumi, a thirteenth century poet,
philosopher, and Sufi mystic.

#ParrotandtheMerchant

First published in the United Kingdom in 2015 by Tiny Owl Publishing Ltd
This edition first published in the United States and the United Kingdom
in 2019 by Tiny Owl Publishing Ltd

www.tinyowl.co.uk

TINY OWL

Translated by Azita Rassi
© 2015 Tiny Owl Publishing Ltd
Text and illustrations © 2013 Chekkeh Publisher, Tehran, Iran

Marjan Vafaeian has asserted her right under the Copyright, Designs and Patents Act
1988 to be identified as the Author and Illustrator of this work.

A catalogue record of this book is available from the British Library.
A CIP record for this book is available from the Library of Congress.

ISBN 978-1-910328-03-3 (Hardback)
ISBN 978-1-910328-25-5 (Paperback)

Printed in Malta

MARJAN VAFAEIAN

The PARROT and the Merchant

A TALE BY RUMI

Long ago in Persia there lived a merchant named Mah Jahan. Mah Jahan went far and wide, buying and selling beautiful things.

The beautiful things that Mah Jahan collected for herself on her journeys were beautiful birds. She kept them in cages or chains so that they couldn't fly away and leave her.

Mah Jahan's most precious bird of all was a
beautiful bright parrot that she had brought back
from India. She loved that parrot best of all her birds
because the parrot had learned to talk.

Mah Jahan was about to go and trade in India again. She asked her servants, "What would you like me to bring you back as a gift?" Each of them told her what they wanted.

Then Mah Jahan went to see her parrot. She said, "Tell me what I can bring you to make you happy."

The parrot put its head on one side. Then it said, "Please say hello to my parrot friends in India. Tell them that I miss them, and that makes me sad.

Ask them if they have any advice for me."

"I will," promised Mah Jahan.

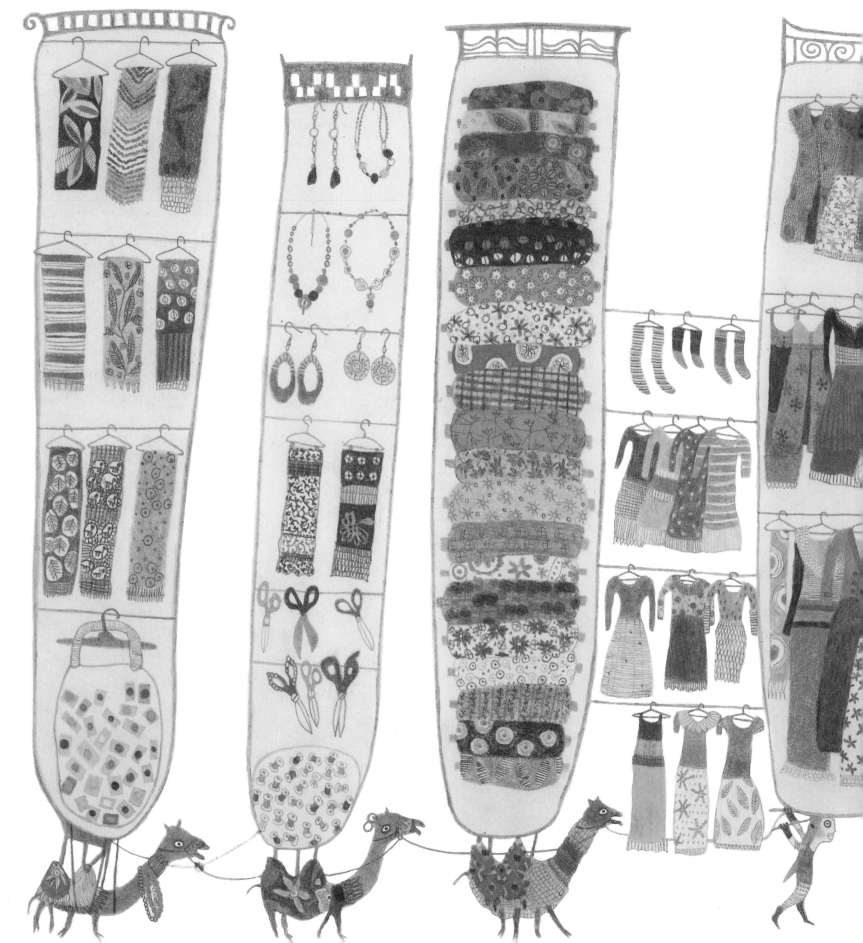

Mah Jahan bid goodbye to her servants and her birds, and she and her workers set off with a caravan of camels loaded with goods to be traded.

In India, Mah Jahan sold all that she had brought from Persia, and she bought Indian goods to sell when she got home. She bought the gifts for her servants.

Mah Jahan was packed and ready to head back home when she remembered the promise that she had made to her parrot. So Mah Jahan went into the Indian jungle where parrots lived wild and free.

"Dear parrots," said Mah Jahan. "I have a message for you from my parrot at home. She says to tell you that she misses you very much, and, please, have you any advice that could make her happy?"

These wild parrots didn't say anything in a language that a person could understand. But suddenly one of them went very still, then dropped from the tree.

Oh, how terrible, that parrot has just died! thought Mah Jahan, and she hurried away from the jungle.

In the days it took to travel home, Mah Jahan didn't know whether to tell her parrot about her friend who died in the jungle. It would make her even more sad, she thought.

When she got home Mah Jahan gave the presents she had promised to her servants, but she said nothing to her parrot until he asked, "Mistress, what did my parrot friends tell you?"

Mah Jahan decided to answer, "I'm afraid that they said nothing at all, but one poor parrot fell out of the tree, dead."

Mah Jahan's parrot said nothing, but after a moment it too suddenly went still, and it dropped to the floor of its cage.

Oh, no! thought Mah Jahan. *I have made my parrot die of sadness!* She opened the door of the parrot's cage, and she gently took the still parrot in her hands, and she wept.

But then the parrot moved! It twisted onto its feet,
shook the dust off its wings, and flew up into the air.

"Oh!" said Mah Jahan. "You're alive!"

The parrot sat on a branch of a tree.
"I am more alive than I have been since
you caged me, Mistress! Thank you, thank you
for the gift of freedom that you brought me
from India!"

"But I only brought you a sad story," said Mah Jahan.

"It was a story sent by my friends to teach me how to escape," said the parrot. "They showed what I must do to become happy! Goodbye, Mistress!"

And then the parrot flew away, home to India.

Mah Jahan was surprised to find that she was happy to lose her parrot to freedom. That is because I truly do love that parrot, she thought.

About the book

The Parrot and the Merchant is a timeless story, written
800 years ago, still relevant for modern readers.
The illustrations are a sophisticated mix of beautiful birds and fabrics
with interestingly strange, almost sinister, human characters. There's
a lot in this fable for readers to think about and discuss. This book
could be the starting point for children to create their own simple
stories to demonstrate a universal truth. And the illustrations might
well prompt readers to develop their own visual story ideas.

About the author and illustrator

Rumi was a thirteenth century poet, philosopher, and mystic whose
works have been studied for centuries, and still speak to us today.
Some of his songs have been put to music by contemporary
Western artists, and now this book brings a wise story about
true love into the English language in book form.

Award-winning Iranian illustrator, **Marjan Vafaeian,** has brought a
modern twist to this ancient fable, casting a woman as the merchant.